Click, Clack, Boo!

For Rose M. —D. C.
For Gaby —B. L.

SIMON SPOTLIGHT
An imprint of Simon & Schuster Children's Publishing Division
1230 Avenue of the Americas, New York, New York 10020
This Simon Spotlight edition July 2018
Text copyright © 2013 by Doreen Cronin
Illustrations copyright © 2013 by Betsy Lewin
For information about special discounts for bulk purchases, please contact Simon & Schuster Special Sales at
1-866-506-1949 or business@simonandschuster.com.
Manufactured in the United States of America 0618 LAK
2 4 6 8 10 9 7 5 3 1
Cataloging-in-Publication Data is available from the Library of Congress.
ISBN 978-1-5344-1380-1 (hc)
ISBN 978-1-5344-1379-5 (pbk)
ISBN 978-1-5344-1381-8 (eBook)

Click, Clack, Boo!

A tricky treat

Doreen Cronin *and* **Betsy Lewin**

Ready-to-Read

Simon Spotlight

New York London Toronto Sydney New Delhi

Farmer Brown does not like
Halloween.

Witches give him nightmares.

Pirates give him shivers.

Jack-o'-lanterns flicker
spooky shadows on the wall.

Farmer Brown leaves a bowl of candy on the porch.

He puts up a DO NOT DISTURB sign.
He draws the shades
and locks the door.

But in the barn
the Halloween party
has just begun.

There is a
crunch,
crunch,
crunching
as the mice scurry across the field.

There is a
creak,
   creak,
creaking
as the sheep slowly push open
the barn door.

There is a
tap,
tap,
tapping,
and the cows go to the window
to let the cats in.

Farmer Brown does not like the
sounds of Halloween night.
He checks the lock on the door.
He peeks through the window.

There is a dark creature
standing beneath
the trees.

Farmer Brown runs to his room,
pulls on his pajamas,
and climbs under the covers.

He hears the
crunch,
    crunch,
crunching
of leafy footsteps
heading toward the house.

There is a
creak,
creak,
creaking
on the old boards
of the front porch.

Then a
**tap,
tap,
tapping**
on the front door.

Farmer Brown pulls up
his covers tight.
He hears a
quack,
    quack,
quackle
in the crisp night air.

Quackle??

Farmer Brown jumps out of bed.

The porch is empty.
The candy bowl is gone.

There is a new note
on Farmer Brown's door:

HALLOWEEN
PARTY
at the barn!

Farmer Brown runs to the barn.

There is a **creak,**
creak,
creaking
on the old boards
of the front porch . . .

and a **crunch, crunch, crunching** of leafy footsteps heading toward the barn.

There is a **tap,**
tap,
tapping
on the window.

Happy Halloween!